Lost and Found

HIGHLIGHTS PRESS
Honesdale, Pennsylvania

Cracker, Jack

Polly wants the path from START to FINISH.

START

FINISH

Illustrated by Rob Sepanak

Woodworker

Terry the termite is planning to eat his way through the entire house. Which trail will take Terry to the top?

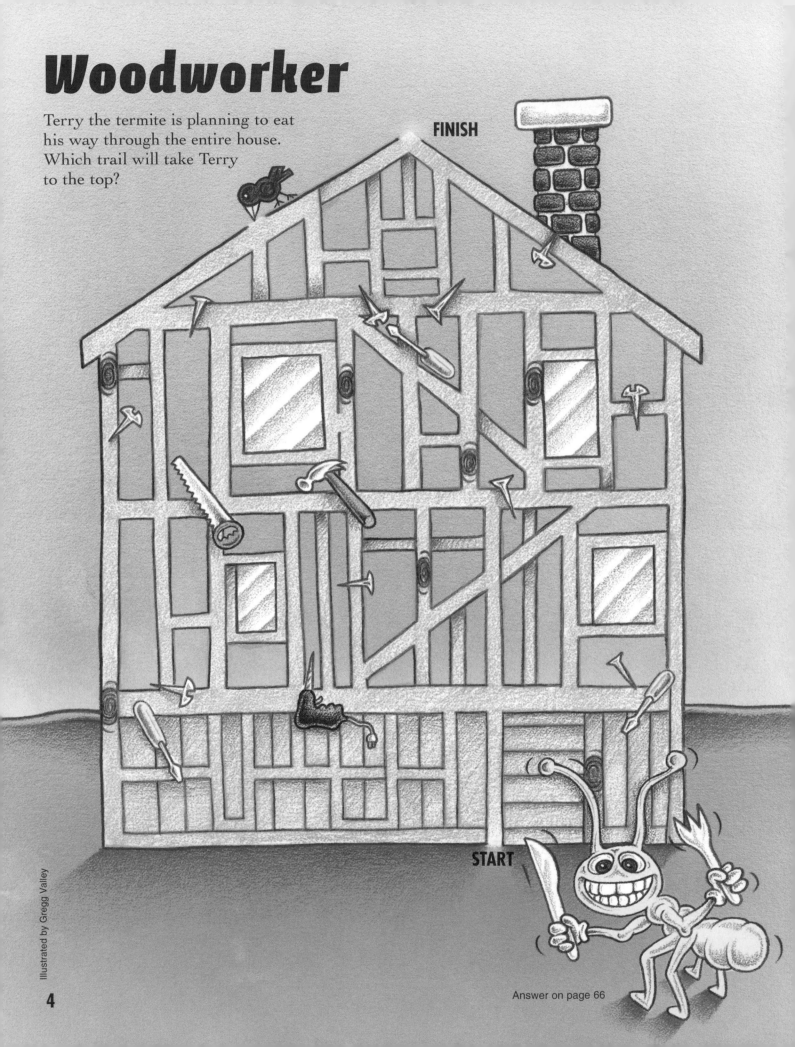

FINISH

START

4

Answer on page 66

Pecos Bill

Start in the center and ride the wildest wind in
the Wild West to get Bill back to his saddle.

Answer on page 66

FINISH

Illustrated by Marc Nadel

Bunny Run

Help the bunny slalom down the hill and cross the finish line.

START

Illustrated by Jeff George

FINISH

Answer on page 66

START

FINISH

Creepy Canyon Maze

Idaho Murphy has to get across this canyon, but the bridge is out. Can you find another way he can get across?

Answer on page 66.

Illustrated by Marc Nadel

Open Sesame

Can you make it to the welcome mat?

START→

Answer on page 66

Illustrated by Marc Nadel

Coaster Coast

Keep your hands and arms inside the car as you
try to ride from START to FINISH.

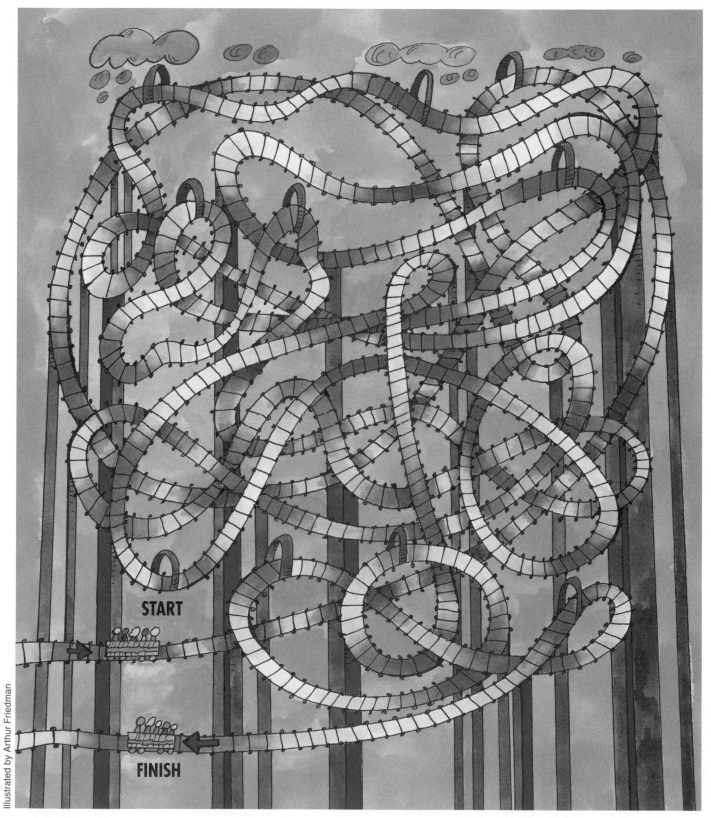

START

FINISH

Answer on page 66

Treasure Quest

These buccaneers are sailing the seven seas in search of a word treasure. On their ancient chart, the numbers below each space show which island to sail to and then what letter the buccaneers want. For example: 1-2 means to sail to island number 1 and to take the second letter from the island's name. So 1-2 will be *A*. See if you can travel through the islands to gather up the letters that will answer the buccaneer question.

What is a buccaneer?

___   ___ ___ ___ ___   ___ ___ ___ ___ ___
1-2   4-1 6-2 2-1 7-4   5-1 8-5 5-2 3-1 4-5

___ ___ ___   ___ ___ ___ ___
6-1 2-3 7-6   5-3 3-3 4-3 7-2

Illustrated by John Nez

1. Palm

2. Ghost

10

Answer on page 66

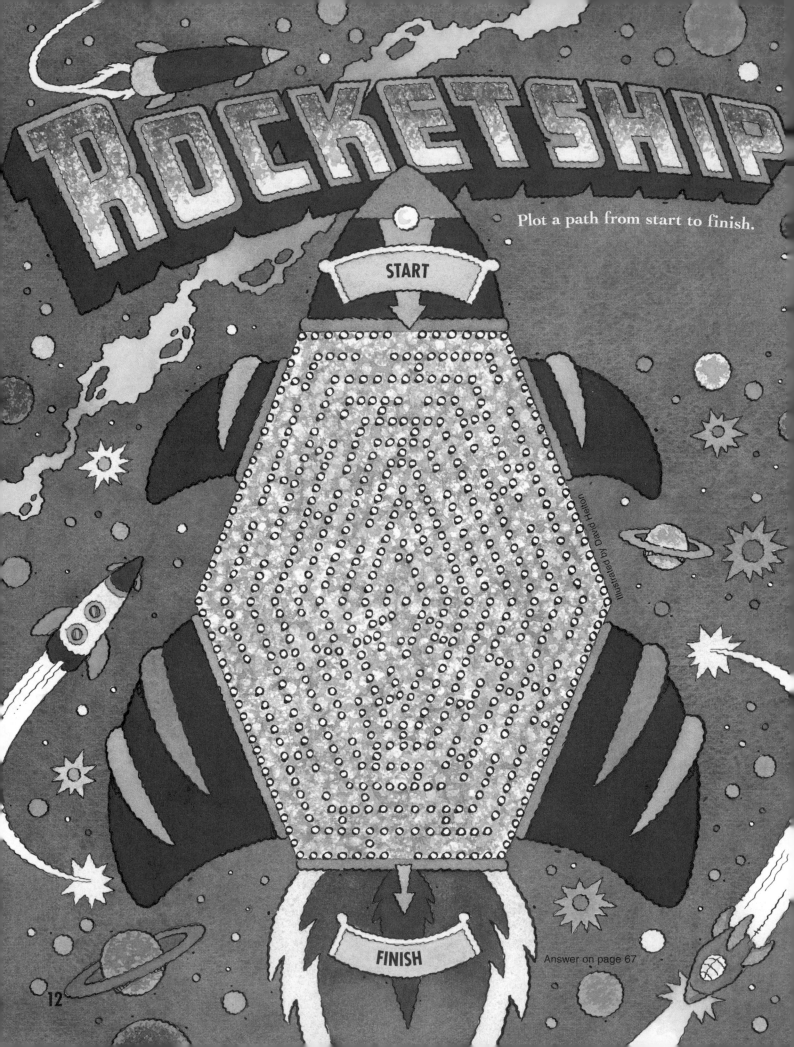

Pyramid of Peril

Help this explorer find the one path that will safely lead him to all three statues and out to the sun. Don't double back or cross your path or you may fall victim to the dangers of the pyramid.

START

FINISH

Illustrated by Mark Stash

Answer on page 67

A Dirty Job

This machine seemed like a good idea at first. It allowed four people to vacuum a room at the same time. However, these testers got all tangled up so that some reworking needs to be done. Can you figure out which lettered hose goes to which tester?

Illustrated by John Killgrew

14

Answer on page 67

Cookie Cutups

Work your way around the tray to find out who gets the most cookies.

Illustrated by Arieh Zeldich

Answer on page 67

Garden Maze

While on vacation, you find this lovely garden maze. You've been lost in it for hours. Find the one path that leads out.

Illustrated by Marc Nadel

Out with the Tide

Untangle this mess by following the ropes to the pylons so each ship can be untied and sail out to the open sea.

Illustrated by Jerry Zimmerman

Answer on page 67

One Up

Marty Megabyte is a mathematical master. But he isn't too magnificent at mazes. Help him work his way through this maze by going up only one number in each sum. For example: 0+1=1. From there, move to 1+1, which equals 2. Next, look for a block that equals 3, and so on. Look up, down, across, backwards, or diagonally. Hints: The sums will only increase, not decrease. The correct path has fifteen steps between IN and OUT.

10 x 0	3 x 3 − 2	12 − 2 + 1	3 x 4	5 x 3 − 2
16 − 6	11 + 3 − 7	1 + 2 + 3 + 4	20 + 4 + 6	2 + 3 + 4 + 5
18 + 2 − 88	4 x 2 + 3	0 x 11	10 − 5 + 4	15 x 1 → OUT
12 − 2 + 5	6 x 1 x 2	4 x 2 + 8	4 x 2	17 − 7 + 5
8 − 4 + 1	3 + 2 + 1	9 − 2	18 + 9	10 − 4
9 + 3	10 ÷ 2	7 − 7	1 + 2 + 3	3 x 3
7 − 6 + 1	2 + 2	5 − 3	8 + 4	1 + 4
4 − 3	1 x 0	3 x 1	6 − 5	2 + 2
IN → 0 + 1	1 + 1	2 + 0	3 x 0	10 − 8

Turtle Puzzle

Which path will lead one
tiny turtle to the lettuce?

Answer on page 67

FINISH

START

Root Route

Truffle hunters Trevor and Troy are tracking down the world's tastiest treat, the Trupnik Truffle. Trace the trail that will make them triumphant.

Illustrated by Marc Nadel

Bee-cause!

Help the bees find their
way into the chamber
where the honey is stored.
Start at the arrow.

Answer on page 68

HONEY

Illustrated by Judith Hunt

Year of the Dragons

You will be fortunate indeed if you can tell what color each numbered dragon is about to be painted. Track back along the scales to go from each number to the tail.

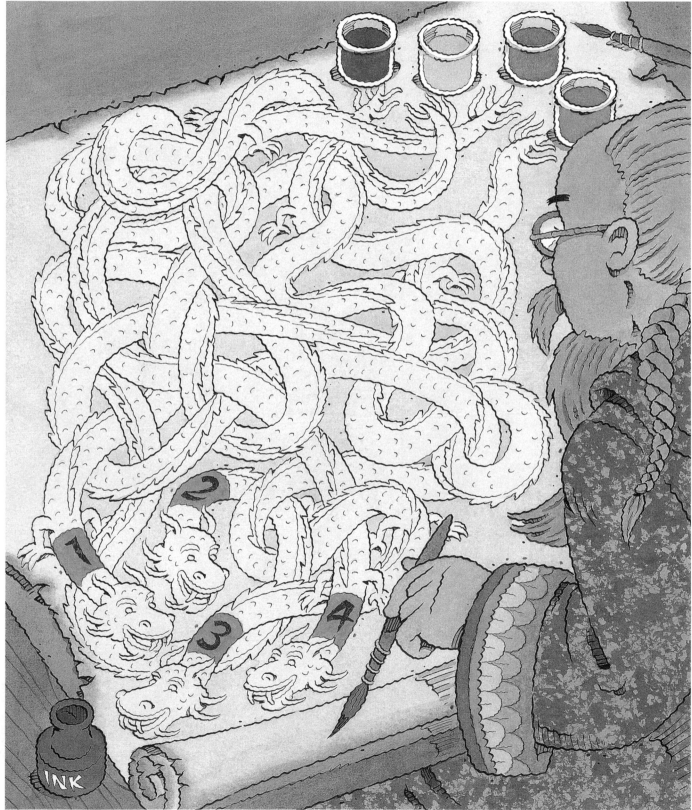

Illustrated by David Helton

Answer on page 68

Float Your Boat

Sail from the mainland to the island by navigating only through water vessels.
If you bump into a land vessel, you'll sink and have to start over.

Wagon

Barge

Yacht

Barge

Bicycle

Moped

Canoe

Raft

Trolley

Sloop

Kayak

Pickup

Bus

Truck

Car

Cutter

Answer on page 68

Proud Portrait

Terence is trying to clean his pop's portrait. But the timid tiger is too shy to give that spider the brush-off. Help the spider find a path from the nose back up to the spider web in time for Terence to finish cleaning. The spider won't cross over any lines on either the portrait or frame.

Illustrated by Arieh Zeldich

Answer on page 68

Cave at Emptor

You should have been more careful when you bought your ticket for this ride. Now you're stuck between the stalagmites of Emptor Cave. You can see the exit, but can you find your way there?

Illustrated by Lynn Adams

START

FINISH

Bats!

Boris badly wants to beat his brothers to the belfry. You can help him fly right by showing him what path to stake out.

START

FINISH

Illustrated by Arthur Friedman

Answer on page 68

Pond Ponder

Fritzi Frog was on the far side of the pond when it began to rain.
Now there are triple ripples on the water. Help Fritzi find a way
to wade through the surging circles. Answer on page 68

START

FINISH

Bow-Wow Boaters

Follow the ropes to match each "hot dog" skier to a barking boater.

Illustrated by R. Michael Palan

Answer on page 68

Magic Spell

A miller's daughter is spinning straw into gold, thanks to the secret help of a mystical little man. Now she has to guess his name or he'll tell the king the truth. If she looks carefully, she'll see the name woven into a path leading from the spinning wheel to him. Can you spell it out for her?

Illustrated by Marc Nadel

Answer on page 69

Jungle Gym

Quit monkeying around and help Tarzan find the path down to little Kreegah.

START

FINISH

Answer on page 69

Illustrated by T. F. Cook

Help these space miners dig their way to the center of Asteroid X-237.

Answer on page 69

Illustrated by David Helton

Weight a Second!

If you weighed 98 pounds and were carrying three one-pound bowling pins, and you had to cross a bridge that would hold only 100 pounds, how could you do it?

Each line will lead you from a letter to a
blank space. Write the letter in the blank space.
When you are finished, you'll have the answer.

34

Answer on page 69

Hang On Tight

This maze has its ups and downs, but see if you can find the one path from top to bottom.

START

Illustrated by Charles Jordan

Answer on page 69

Malt Maze

Can you slurp through this malt all the way to the bottom?

START

FINISH

Illustrated by Charles Jordan

Answer on page 69

Minus Maze

To find your way through this maze, subtract the first pair of numbers (6-1). Draw a line to the answer (5), then move to the next pair of numbers and do the same. Answers may be to the left, right, up, or down.

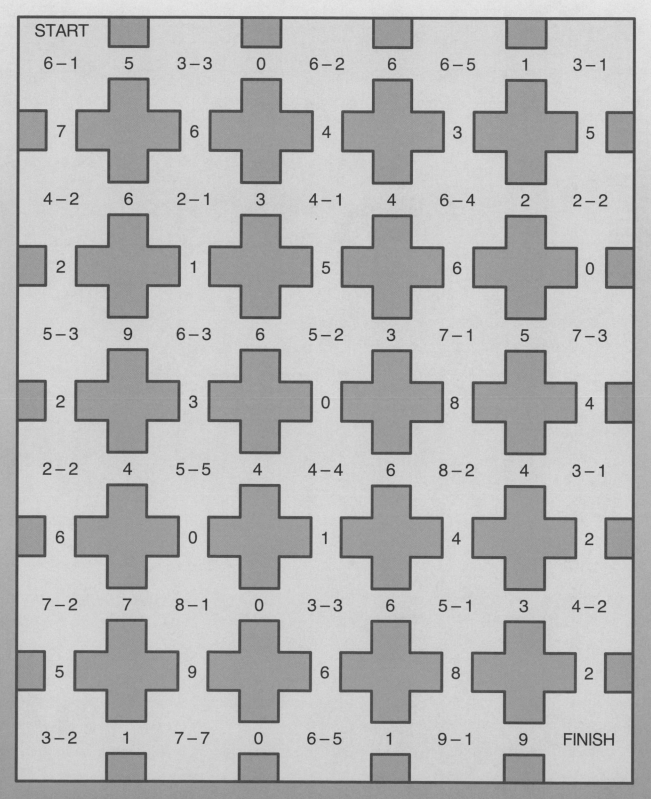

START

6 – 1	5	3 – 3	0	6 – 2	6	6 – 5	1	3 – 1
7				4		3		5
4 – 2	6	2 – 1	3	4 – 1	4	6 – 4	2	2 – 2
2		1		5		6		0
5 – 3	9	6 – 3	6	5 – 2	3	7 – 1	5	7 – 3
2		3		0		8		4
2 – 2	4	5 – 5	4	4 – 4	6	8 – 2	4	3 – 1
6		0		1		4		2
7 – 2	7	8 – 1	0	3 – 3	6	5 – 1	3	4 – 2
5		9		6		8		2
3 – 2	1	7 – 7	0	6 – 5	1	9 – 1	9	FINISH

Answer on page 69

Bee Lines

Three of these bees can move through the maze to the hive. Which one cannot?

Answer on page 69

Illustrated by Lynn Adams

Zigzag Ziggurat

Help Cincinnati Holmes reach
the top of this ancient pyramid.

FINISH

START

Illustrated by John Nez

The Lodge Meeting

The Leave It to Beavers club is having its annual meeting, and Barry Beaver is running late. Can you help him find his way into the lodge before the meeting begins?

FINISH

START

Illustrated by Lynn Adams

Answer on page 70

An Old Maze

Find the path through these ancient drawings that will lead you to hear the music of Kokopelli.

Start

KOKOPELLI

Illustrated by Tom Powers

Answer on page 70

Spy Guy

Sneak past this top spy by finding a path from START to FINISH.

START

FINISH

Illustrated by R. Michael Palan

Answer on page 70

High Flyer

Can you help this bird find a path
through the balloon and the clouds
from START to FINISH?

START

FINISH

Illustrated by Paul Richer

Answer on page 70

All You Need Is Glove . . .

. . . and the one path that will lead through the glove and the ball.

START

FINISH

Illustrated by David Helton

Answer on page 70

Fore!

Pick the path for Percy's putt to plunk into the hole.

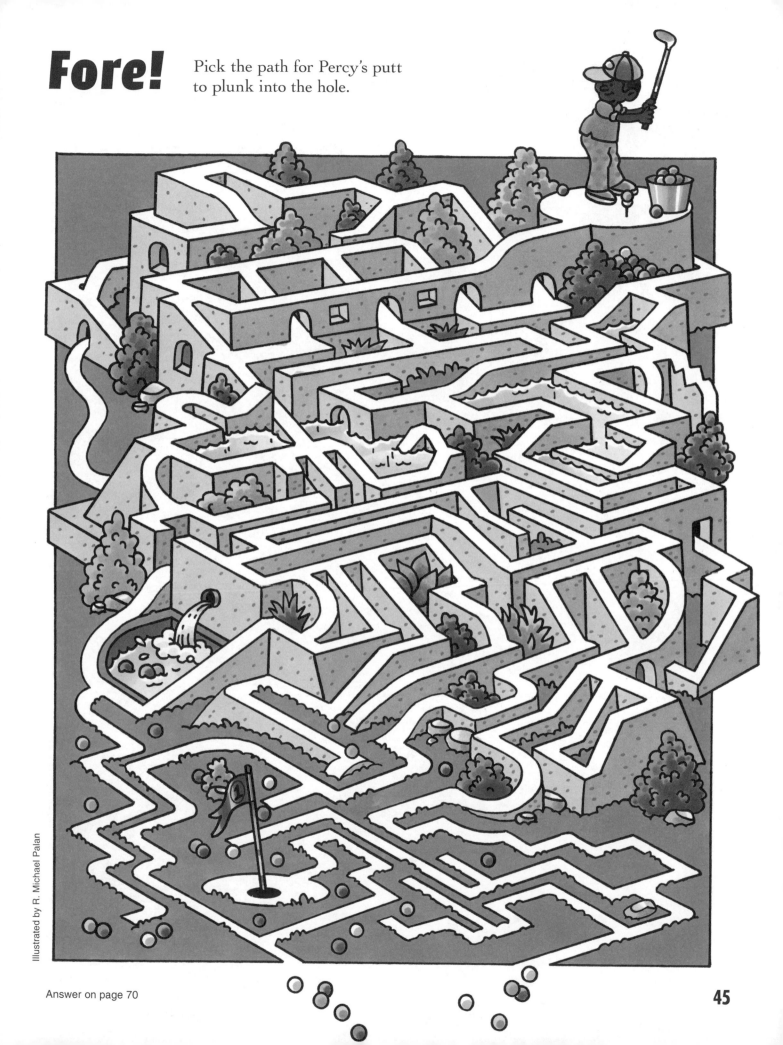

Illustrated by R. Michael Palan

Answer on page 70

Board Walk

START

Buckminster is too full to gnaw through all this lumber. He sees the saw but needs your help to reach it.

FINISH

THE·BEV

46

Answer on page 70

Room to Bloom

Which blossom grew from which plant? Follow the tangled vines to find the answer.

A B C D E

1 2 3 4 5

Answer on page 70

Illustrated by Lynn Adams

Don't Be Chicken

Find a way for Nathan to reach the trough so he can feed these fowl.

START

FEED

FINISH

Illustrated by Frank Bolle

Answer on page 70

A Melody Maze

The music goes round and round, and it comes out where? Help the music flow through this guitar by following the maze from START to FINISH.

START

FINISH

Illustrated by Paul Richer

Answer on page 71

49

Art Works

Can you help this critic climb through to the painting that needs to be straightened?

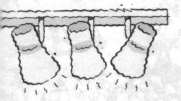

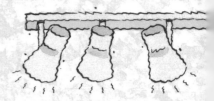

FINISH

START

Illustrated by David Helton

Answer on page 71

Pounding the Pavement

Can you find your way home from the museum before it gets dark?

MUSEUM

START

CAN'T HAIL A TAXI

WRONG TURN

TRAFFIC JAM

DETOUR

LOST IN A CROWD

SUBWAY DELAY

DEAD END

MISSED THE TROLLEY

BUS BREAKDOWN

HOME SWEET HOME

Illustrated by Paul Richer

Answer on page 71

Dino Draw

Can you find the path around and through this dozing dino?

START

FINISH

Answer on page 71

Reindeer Games

Can you help Herbie find which reindeer or pair of reindeer is tied to each lead?

Illustrated by Jeff Shelly

Answer on page 71

Castle Cutaway

You'll rule this kingdom if you can find the one path from the tower to the gateway.

START

FINISH

Answer on page 71

Illustrated by Marc Nadel

Going Batty

Lead Lawrence through this labyrinth to the opening above.

FINISH

START

Illustrated by R. Michael Palan

Answer on page 71

Beauty and the Beast

You'll be doing beautifully if you can find your way through this beastly maze.

Answer on page 71

START

Illustrated by Marc Nadel

FINISH

Cat's Up

Can you find the path that will help Big Ed reach Fluffy?

FINISH

START

Answer on page 72

Eye See

The Fabulous Parroti Brothers have painted a new masterpiece. Can you follow their uninterrupted brushstrokes to see who painted this zebra's eye?

Illustrated by Arieh Zeldich

Answer on page 72

Eggshell Eggscapees

All the animals below really do hatch from eggs.
Can you tell which animal hatched from which egg?

Illustrated by Charles Jordan

Answer on page 72

Mayan Maze

This mighty maze was discovered in some ancient ruins. Will you be the first explorer to find a way out?

START

Answer on page 72

Maze-terpiece

To reveal the subject of this painting, trace a path that begins and ends at the artist's brush without crossing any brushstrokes.

Illustrated by Marc Nadel

END

START

Down on the Farm

Farmer Brown has left bags of seed out in the middle of the field. Help him find his way through the rows to the seed.

Answer on page 72

Illustrated by Judith Hunt

SEED

SEED

SUN FARM

63

Measuring Up

Can you tell which builder is using which tape measure?

Illustrated by Mark Corcoran

Answer on page 72

Build-a-Bike Maze

Danny and Mr. Fix-it want to build a bicycle. Help them by picking up all the bicycle parts on Danny's list as you travel through the junkyard.

List on scroll:
- HANDLE-BARS
- SEAT
- WHEEL
- FENDERS
- PEDALS
- CHAIN
- MIRROR
- HORN
- REFLECTOR
- FRAME

START→

FINISH

Illustrated by Judith Hunt

Answer on page 72

Answers

Cover

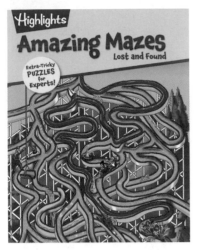

Page 3 Cracker, Jack

Page 4 Woodworker

Page 5 Pecos Bill

Page 6 Bunny Run

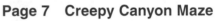

Page 7 Creepy Canyon Maze

Page 8 Open Sesame

Page 9 Coaster Coast

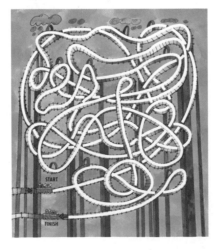

Pages 10–11 Treasure Quest

What is a buccaneer?

A	H	I	G	H
1-2	4-1	6-2	2-1	7-4

P	R	I	C	E
5-1	8-5	5-2	3-1	4-5

F	O	R
6-1	2-3	7-6

C	O	R	N
5-3	3-3	4-3	7-2

Page 12   Rocket Ship

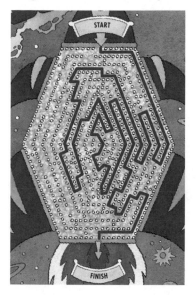

Page 13   Pyramid of Peril

Page 14   A Dirty Job

1 – D
2 – A
3 – B
4 – C

Page 15   Cookie Cutups

Pinwheels – 22
Circles – 21
Hexagons – 18

Pages 16–17   Garden Maze

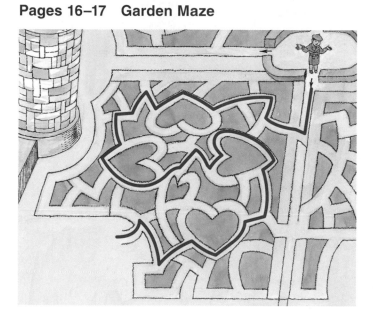

Page 18   Out with the Tide

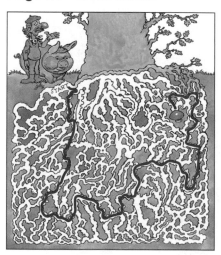

Page 19   One Up

Page 20   Turtle Puzzle

Page 21   Root Route

Page 22   Bee-cause!

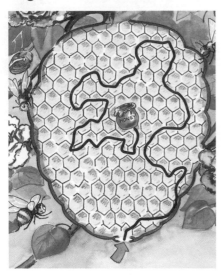

Page 23   Year of the Dragons

1–Green   3–Red
2–Blue   4–Yellow

Page 24   Float Your Boat

Page 25   Proud Portrait

Pages 26–27   Cave at Emptor

Page 28   Bats!

Page 29   Pond Ponder

Page 30   Bow-Wow Boaters

1–C
2–A
3–D
4–B

Page 31   Magic Spell

Page 32   Jungle Gym

Page 33   X-237

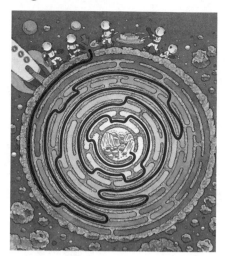

Page 34   Weight a Second!

JUGGLE THEM

Page 35   Hang On Tight

Page 36   Malt Maze

Page 37   Minus Maze

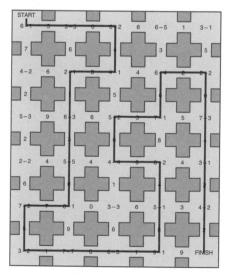

Page 38   Bee Lines

Bee number 4 cannot reach the hive.

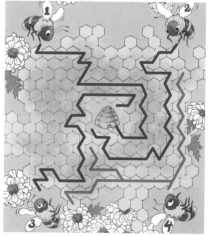

Page 39   Zigzag Ziggurat

Page 40   The Lodge Meeting

Page 41   An Old Maze

Page 42   Spy Guy

Page 43   High Flyer

Page 44   All You Need Is Glove . . .

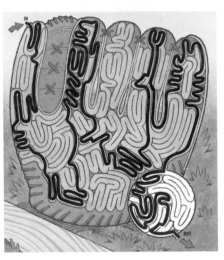

Page 45   Fore!

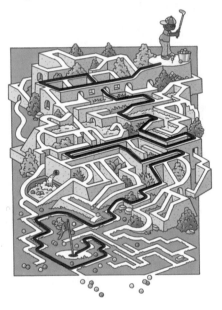

Page 46   Board Walk

Page 47   Room to Bloom

A–3   B–5   C–4
D–2   E–1

Page 48   Don't Be Chicken

Here is one possible solution. You may have found others.

Page 49   A Melody Maze

Page 50   Art Works

Page 51   Pounding the Pavement

Page 52   Dino Draw

Page 53   Reindeer Games

1—D/B   2—R   3—C/C
4—D/D   5—P/V

Page 54   Castle Cutaway

Page 55   Going Batty

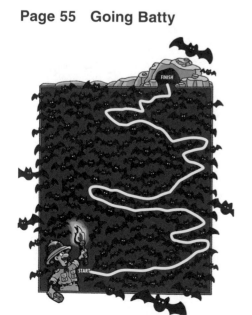

Pages 56–57   Beauty and the Beast

Page 58   Cat's Up

Page 59   Eye See

The red parrot painted the zebra's eye.

Page 60   Eggshell Eggscapees

1—C   2—A   3—D   4—B

Page 61   Mayan Maze

Page 62   Maze-terpiece

Page 63   Down on the Farm

Page 64   Measuring Up

1—B   2—C   3—A   4—D

Page 65   Build-a-Bike Maze